Animal Tales from
Panchatantra

Wonder House

Printed 2019

Wonder House
(An imprint of Prakash Books Pvt. Ltd.)

Wonder House Books
Corporate & Editorial Office
113-A, 1st Floor, Ansari Road,
Daryaganj, New Delhi-110002
Tel +91 11 2324 7062-65

ISBN : 978-93-89178-11-1

Printed in India

Contents

About Panchatantra

✿ • • • • • • • • • • • ✿

The Panchatantra is a collection of five books comprising of ancient Indian fables written by Pandit Vishnusharma. It's believed to be composed somewhere in the 3rd century BCE. Panchatantra is based on *Nitishastra*. The word 'Panchatantra' is made of two Sanskrit words 'pancha' (five) and 'ṭantra' (thing). It talks about *mitra bheda* (estrangement of friends), *mitra samprapti* (winning of friends), *kakalukiyam* (of crows and owls), *labdha pranasam* (loss of gains), and *aparikshita karakam* (rash deeds). The work is spread across the globe. It first reached Europe sometime in the 11th century. It existed in various languages like Old Slavonic, German, Spanish, Latin, Greek, French and Czech.

In Franklin Edgerton's words, the Panchatantra is "certainly the most frequently translated literary product of India." The stories are as valid in modern times as they were in the ancient times.

A long time ago...

in ancient India, there was a beautiful kingdom named Mahilaropya. The kingdom was ruled by a king named Amarshakti. He had three sons named Ugrashakti, Bahushakti and Anantashakti. Being a scholar himself, Amarshakti was disappointed with his sons' disinterest in learning. Their laziness and inability to gain knowledge made the king very angry.

One day, he called his ministers to discuss with them the future of his successors.

The king said, "I have called upon you to seek advice on an important matter. The men of learning say that idle sons bring dishonour to their father. And I have three of the laziest sons to worry about. I turn to you for counsel on this."

One of the ministers came forward and advised the King to consult a wise Brahmin, Pandit Vishnu Sharma.

Amarshakti accepted his minister's advice and asked them to summon Vishnu Sharma to the palace.

When the Pandit arrived, the King addressed him, "O gentleman, you must undertake the responsibility of teaching my sons. In return, I will give you a hundred land grants."

Vishnu Sharma smiled, "Oh King, I do not need your lands. Learning can't be purchased with money. I will tutor your sons. Six months from now, your sons will be great scholars. And if they are not, you can order me to change my name!"

From that day onwards, the sons lived with Vishnu Sharma and learned the five books, *The Loss of Friends, The Winning of Friends, Crows and Owls, Loss of Gains,* and *Ill-considered Action,* by heart.

The combination of these five books or the Pentateuch is known as *Panchatantra*. It is a *niti-shastra*, also known as a 'textbook of ethics', which teaches the wise conduct of life. Each wise and witty story in all the five books teaches the harmonious development of humans and the ability to achieve joy by combining friendship, prosperity, security, action and learning. Since olden times, Panchatantra has been regarded as a popular children's guide for solving problems of life and continues to do so even today.

We have selected 6 famous animal stories from the Panchatantra for children. The stories are accompanied with bright and beautiful illustrations to make reading a fun-filled experience for the child.

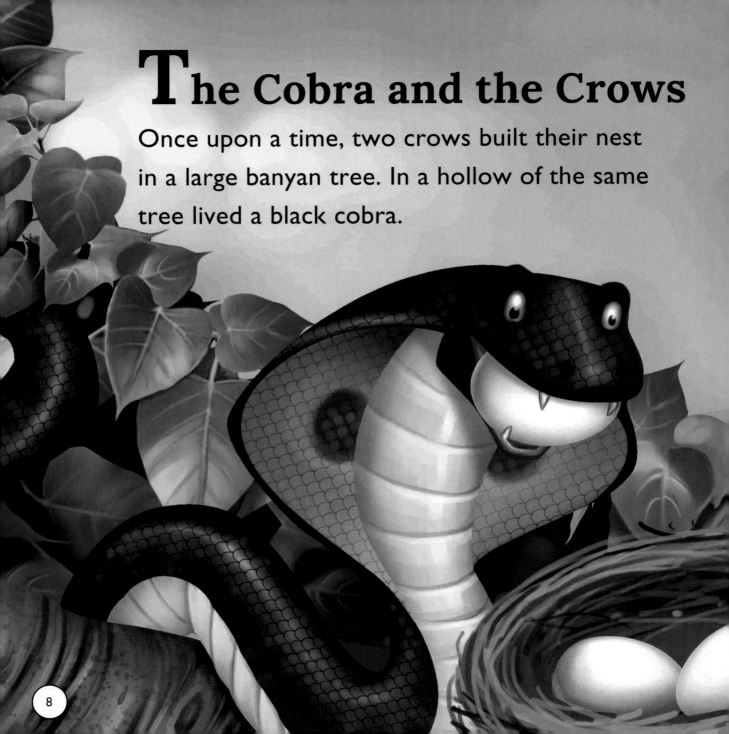

The Cobra and the Crows

Once upon a time, two crows built their nest in a large banyan tree. In a hollow of the same tree lived a black cobra.

Every time the she-crow laid eggs in the nest, the cobra climbed up the tree and ate them. The crows could only watch helplessly.

The grief-stricken crows approached their friend, a jackal, who lived nearby. They narrated their misery to the jackal.

The jackal reassured them, "We can defeat a powerful enemy with the use of wit. I have a plan which can help you get rid of the cobra."

The crows listened carefully and liked
the jackal's plan.

The next day the he-crow flew towards the city. He saw the Queen and her maids bathing in the river.

The crow spotted the Queen's jewels lying on the riverbed. He swooped towards the ground and lifted a pearl necklace. The maids saw the crow stealing the necklace and raised an alarm.

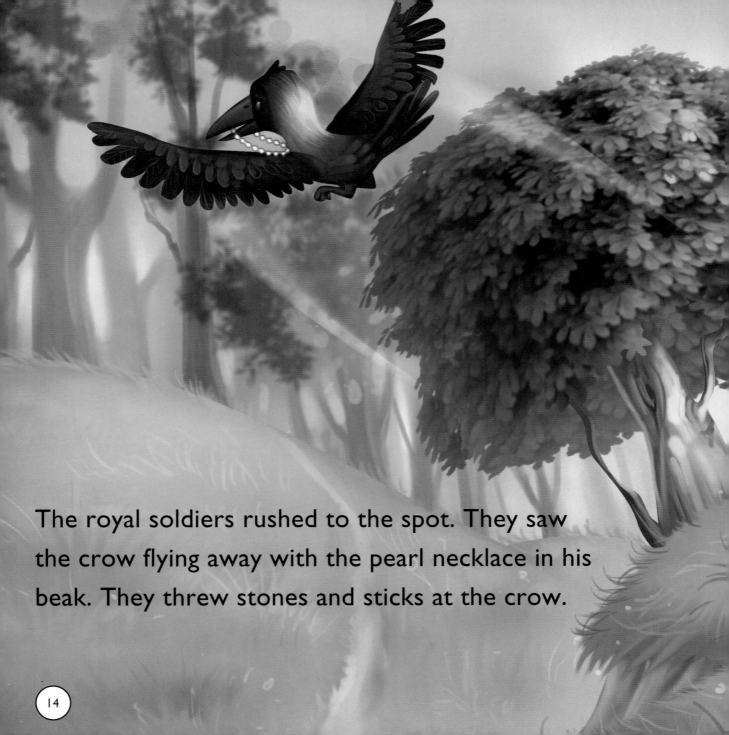

The royal soldiers rushed to the spot. They saw
the crow flying away with the pearl necklace in his
beak. They threw stones and sticks at the crow.

The alert crow avoided them with ease.
He flew slowly to allow the soldiers to follow
him, thus leading them into the forest.

The he-crow flew back to his tree and dropped the
necklace outside the hollow of the tree where the cobra
was fast asleep. He joined the she-crow on the branch of
the tree to draw the attention of the soldiers.

The cobra woke up due to the loud noise made by the crows and came out of the hollow. He was surprised to see the necklace.

When the royal soldiers tried to pick the necklace, the black cobra attacked them with fury. The soldiers attacked the cobra with sticks and stones and killed him.

The soldiers left after recovering the necklace. The crows thanked the jackal for his help.

Moral
A powerful enemy can be
defeated with a clever plan.

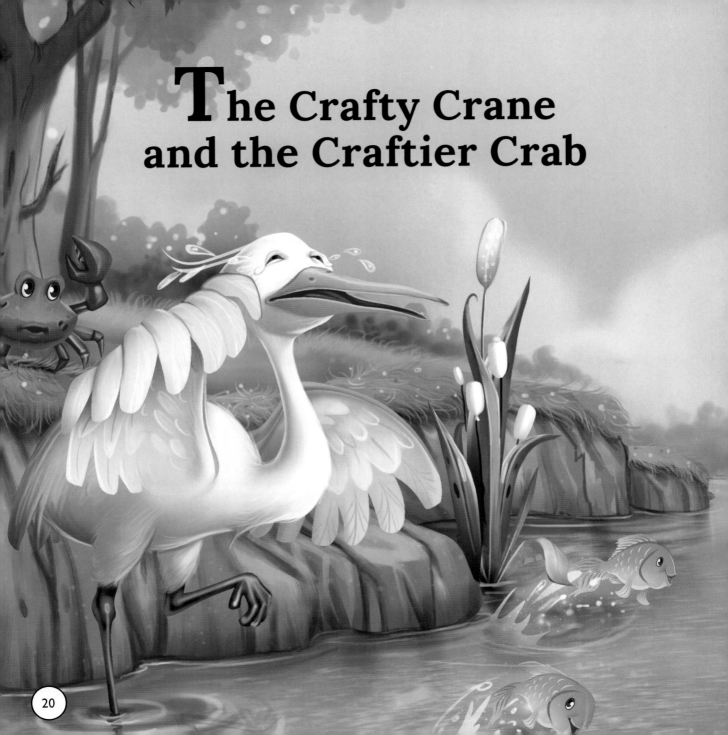

The Crafty Crane and the Craftier Crab

An old crane lived near a huge lake in the jungle.

He was getting weak because he was unable to catch any fish. One day, he stood at the edge of the lake and began weeping. A young crab felt sorry for the crane and asked him, "Why are you crying instead of trying to catching fishes?"

The crane replied, "I have pledged to fast until my death. I will not hunt for fishes anymore."

The crab was curious. "Why are you crying if you plan to renounce the world?"

The crane spoke in a sad voice, "I have heard a prophecy that it won't rain for twelve years. The lake will dry up, and all the fishes living in the lake will die."

The crab was worried. He immediately dived into the lake and conveyed the news to the fishes. The fishes panicked.

The fishes approached the crane along with the crab and pleaded with him to find a solution.

The crane reassured them, "There is no need to panic. There is a huge lake in a faraway land.

It will not dry up even if it doesn't rain for twenty-four years. I can transport you one by one to that lake."

The fishes requested the crane to ferry them to the giant lake. The crane succeeded in his evil plan. Every day the wicked crane would carry a fish from the lake to an isolated spot and smash it against a large rock.

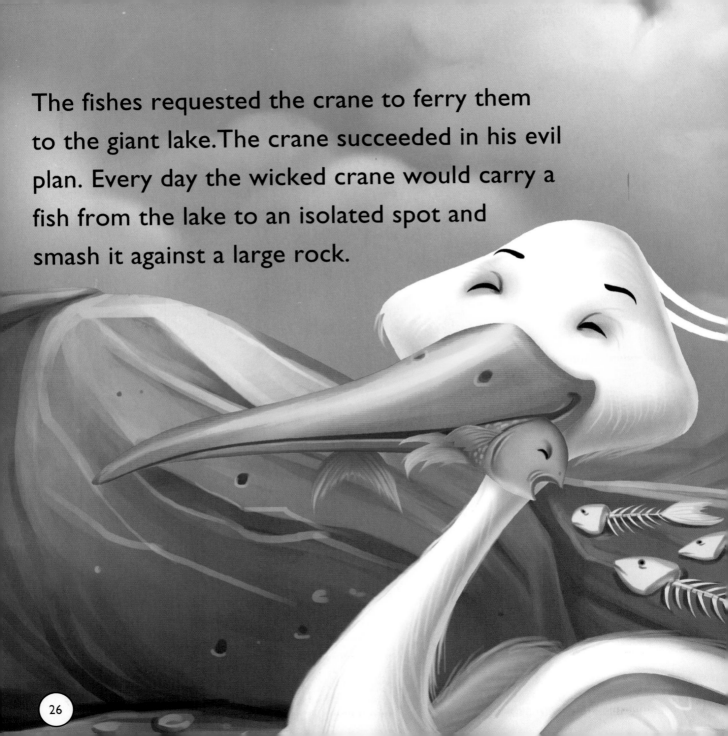

After eating the fish, the crane would return to the lake and convey false stories of how the fishes were happy in their new home. Everyone was eager to go to the beautiful lake.

One day the crab complained to the crane, "You always carry the fishes to the new lake. You never offer to carry me to this beautiful lake."

The crane was happy because he was tired of eating fish. The crab mounted on the crane. As they flew over the large rock, the crab saw the skeletons and understood the evil plan of the crane.

The smart crab spoke innocently, "I am heavy, you must be tired. There is no harm in taking a short rest."

The overconfident crane was sure that the crab could not escape from him while flying. He laughed wickedly and said, "You fool, there is no lake.

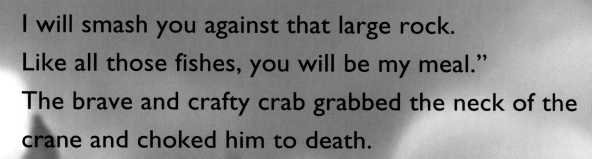

I will smash you against that large rock.
Like all those fishes, you will be my meal."
The brave and crafty crab grabbed the neck of the
crane and choked him to death.

The crab walked back to the lake. The fishes were surprised to see him and asked him the reason for coming back.

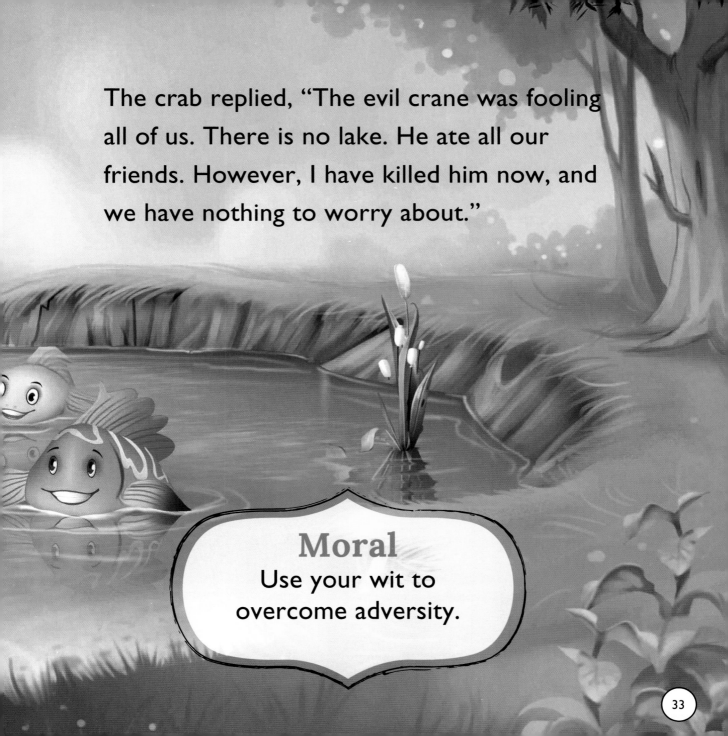

The crab replied, "The evil crane was fooling all of us. There is no lake. He ate all our friends. However, I have killed him now, and we have nothing to worry about."

Moral
Use your wit to overcome adversity.

The Foolish Turtle

Once upon a time, there lived a jolly turtle in a beautiful lake. She had two swans as her good friends. Every day, the three friends would meet near the bank of the lake and narrate stories of their adventures to each other.

They enjoyed each other's company and would
return to their homes only after sunset.

One year, there was no rain, and the
lake began to dry up.

The swans met the turtle and said, "All the water in the lake will dry up soon. We have decided to migrate to a new lake which has plenty of water. We are worried about you. How will you survive here without water?" The turtle was sad and did not want to lose her friends. She begged them to take her along.

The swans said, "You can't fly!
How can we take you with us?"

The turtle thought of a plan and asked the
swans to fetch her a large stick. When the
swans returned with a large stick, the turtle
said, "You can hold the stick on either end
and fly while I hold onto the stick
tightly with my mouth.

Then we can fly to the new lake together."

The swans were sceptical of the plan. They warned the turtle, "Keep your mouth shut at all times. You must not try to speak or you will fall and die."

The turtle promised to keep her mouth shut. Finally, the swans flew up in the air carrying the stick and the turtle with them. The turtle was thrilled to fly with her friends.

As they were flying over a town, the people came out of their houses, staring towards the sky. They shouted, "What a fantastic sight! Those two smart swans are carrying a turtle on a stick."

The turtle was angry as she did not get the credit for her brilliant plan. She opened her mouth to correct them.

The swans watched helplessly as their foolish friend fell on the ground. Children of the town ran towards the turtle and captured her. The sad swans flew away.

Moral
Always listen to the
advice of wise friends.

The Blue Jackal

A stupid jackal lived merrily in the forest.
One day, when he could not find food
in the woods, he sneaked into a
nearby village. A group of dogs
spotted the jackal.

They barked loudly and attacked him.
The jackal fled in panic.

The jackal jumped into a house to escape the dogs, and fell in a big tub filled with blue dye. When he came out of the tub, his entire body had turned blue.

He did not look like an ordinary jackal.

The dogs did not recognise him.
They were scared of the unknown
animal and ran away.

When the jackal did not find any food in the village, he was disappointed and returned to the forest. All the animals of the forest were scared to see a new unknown creature.

The jackal was surprised at their behaviour. He stopped by the pond to drink water. When he saw the blue reflection, he realised that he could use the accident to his advantage.

The jackal called the frightened animals and said, "There is no need to be scared. I am a special messenger of God. I am your new king, and I'm here to protect you."

All the animals accepted the blue jackal as their new king. The blue jackal assigned specific tasks to all the animals.

Every day the lions and tigers
brought food for their new king.

The blue jackal banished all the other jackals from the forest as he did not want them to discover his secret. One day the blue jackal was surrounded by his servants when he heard a pack of jackals howling.

Unable to control his natural instinct, the blue jackal began to howl. He was thrilled to respond to the howls of other jackals.

All the animals realised that the blue jackal had tricked them. He was an ordinary jackal and no messenger of God! They attacked him and drove him out of the forest.

The Cunning Hare and the Foolish Lion

A mighty lion, the king of the jungle, lived on the edge of a forest. He was cruel, and killed animals mercilessly, even when he wasn't hungry.

All the animals of the forest were terrified of the lion. One day, they held a meeting and decided to approach the lion with their grievance.

The unhappy animals formed a union and approached the lion. "Oh, Lord. You don't need to kill animals every day. We will send one animal to you daily for your meal if you promise to stop hunting."

The lion replied, "I agree to your proposal. But I will start killing again if you don't keep your promise."

The relieved animals went back to their homes. The lion kept his promise and stopped hunting. The animals began to roam freely in the forest.

Every day the animals would assemble and
send an unlucky animal to the lion for his meal.
Finally, it was the turn of an intelligent rabbit.

On his way to the lion's cave, he spotted a
well. Suddenly, an idea struck him.

The lion was angry and roared when he saw the rabbit. "How dare they send me a small rabbit? Why are you so late? I am hungry! Now I will kill everyone."

The clever rabbit replied, "Your Majesty, my three friends and I were coming to your cave when another lion sprang out of his den. He claimed that he is the new king of the jungle. He has kept my friends hostage and has challenged you to a duel."

The angry lion ordered the rabbit, "Take me to my enemy. I will kill him and retain my kingdom." The smart rabbit took the lion to the well and said, "Your enemy lives inside this fort."

The lion peeped into the well and saw his reflection, and mistook it for another lion. His roar echoed loudly. The lion jumped inside the well to attack his reflection.

The lion drowned inside the well and died. All the
animals of the forest rejoiced at the death of the
lion and thanked the rabbit for saving their lives.

The Lion that Sprang to Life

Four young Brahmin friends lived in a city in ancient India. Three of them were well versed in all the holy scriptures but lacked common sense. The fourth Brahmin was not learned but was very smart.

One day, they decided to go to the royal court to seek grants from the king.

The four Brahmins set out for the capital of the kingdom. As they were travelling through a forest, they saw the bones of a lion scattered on the ground.

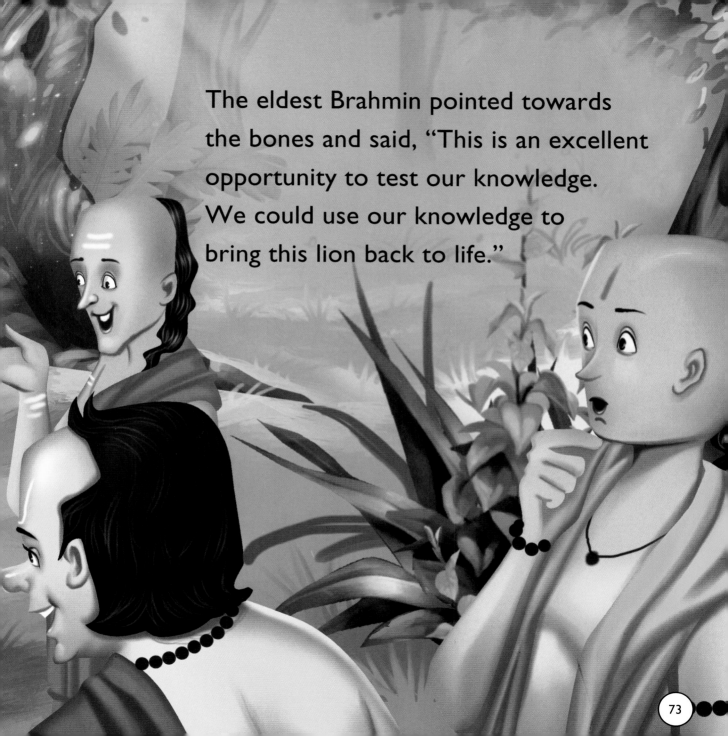

The eldest Brahmin pointed towards the bones and said, "This is an excellent opportunity to test our knowledge. We could use our knowledge to bring this lion back to life."

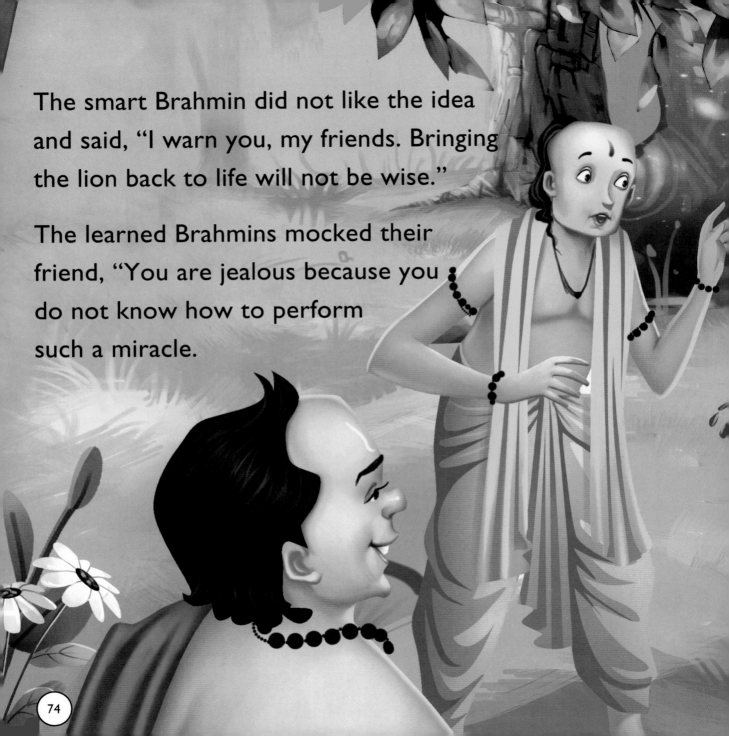

The smart Brahmin did not like the idea and said, "I warn you, my friends. Bringing the lion back to life will not be wise."

The learned Brahmins mocked their friend, "You are jealous because you do not know how to perform such a miracle.

We cannot let an excellent opportunity to test our skills pass."

The eldest Brahmin sat on the ground and rearranged all the scattered bones to form a proper skeleton of the lion.

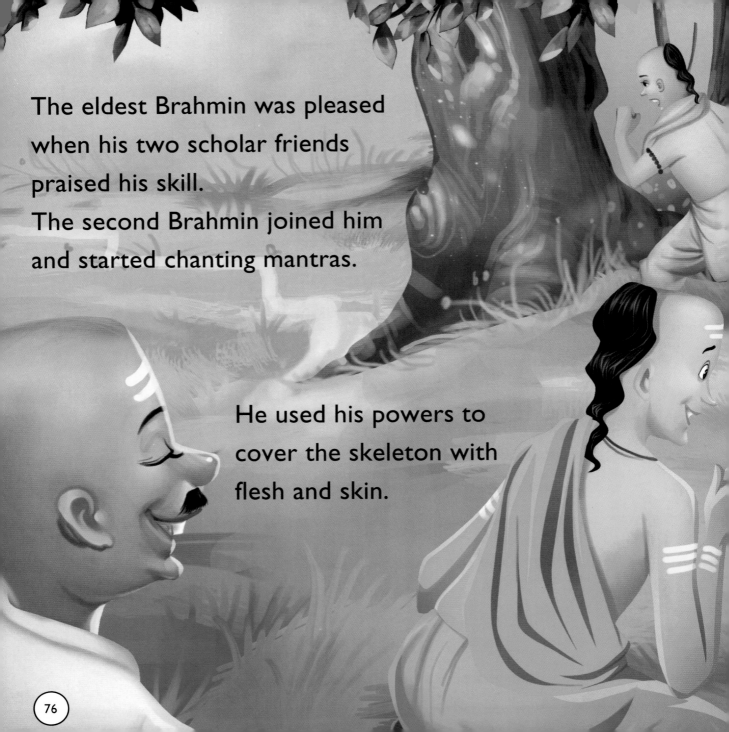

The eldest Brahmin was pleased when his two scholar friends praised his skill.
The second Brahmin joined him and started chanting mantras.

He used his powers to cover the skeleton with flesh and skin.

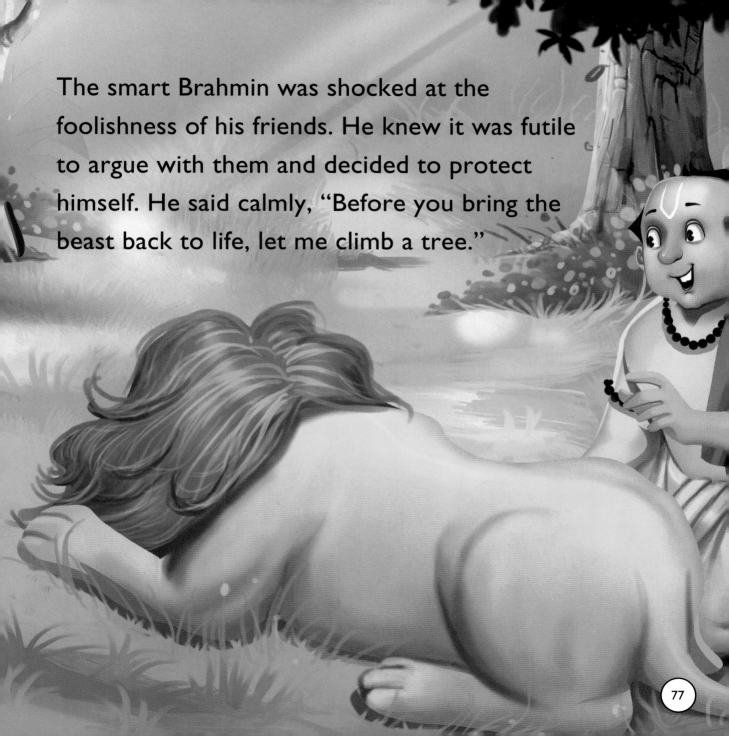

The smart Brahmin was shocked at the foolishness of his friends. He knew it was futile to argue with them and decided to protect himself. He said calmly, "Before you bring the beast back to life, let me climb a tree."

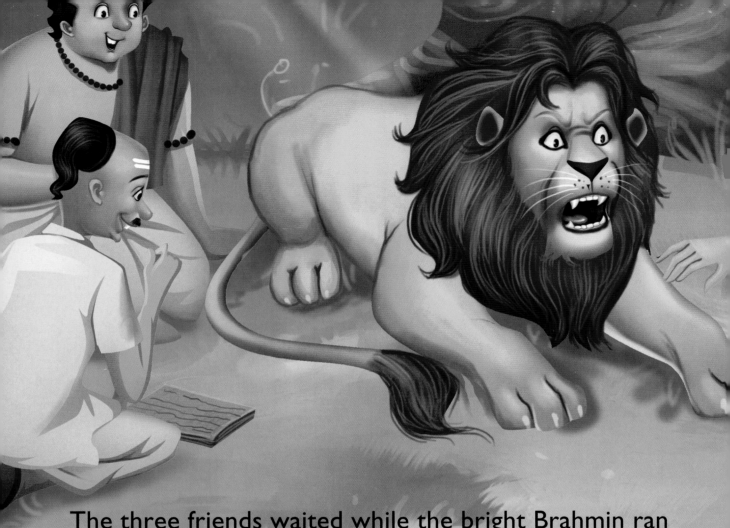

The three friends waited while the bright Brahmin ran
to the nearest tree and climbed up a high branch.

The third Brahmin joined his friends. He sat down
near the dead lion and began the incantation.

Finally, he recited a powerful mantra to give life to the dead lion. The three friends were pleased and boasted about their knowledge when the lion came alive and roared.

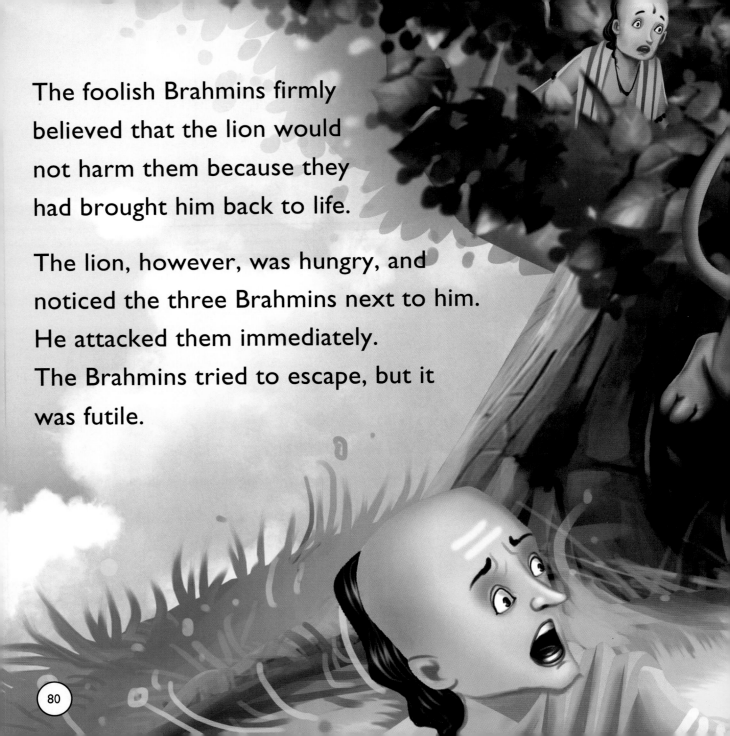

The foolish Brahmins firmly believed that the lion would not harm them because they had brought him back to life.

The lion, however, was hungry, and noticed the three Brahmins next to him. He attacked them immediately. The Brahmins tried to escape, but it was futile.

The clever Brahmin sitting
on the tree watched
in horror as the lion
pounced upon all his
friends and killed them.

The clever Brahmin sat quietly on the tree until he was sure that the lion had gone deep into the forest. He mourned the death of his foolish friends and returned home.

Moral
Common sense is always superior to knowledge.

The End